A Touch Of Smoke And Snow

By Kristy Nicolle

An Ashen Touch Short Story

First published by Kristy Nicolle, United Kingdom, March 2019

QUEENS OF FANTASY EDITION (1st Edition)

Published March 2019 by: Kristy Nicolle

Edited by: Jaimie Cordall

Adult Paranormal/Fantasy Romance

Disclaimer:

This ebook is written in U.K English by personal preference of the author. This is a work of fiction. Names, characters, businesses, places, events and incidents are either the products of the author's imagination or used in a fictitious manner. Any resemblance to actual persons, living or dead, or actual events is purely coincidental.

ISBN: 978-1-911395-19-5

www.kristynicolle.com

For my reader group,
who loved Sephy and Xion from the very first word.

A TOUCH OF SMOKE AND SNOW

XION

30th of November 1995

I arrive, baptised by the cold winter air and the scent of wintergreen. My nostrils flare as I exit the whirling Hollow portal, singed cool by the sudden sensory assault of the surrounding winter dusk. Trees cast shadows long across my form as weak, low-hanging sunlight pushes through the undeniable cracks in the slate grey cloud overhead. My palm throbs, blood clotting within the confines of the cut I made only moments before.

I haven't felt the air this fresh, the greenery this alive in months, and I tense, muscles becoming steel beneath my leather jacket as I brace against my immersion in the mortal world after so long in Mortaria.

Snow crunches underfoot, a light peppering that's salted the underbrush, turning it hard and abrasive as I weave my way through the thick forest at the edge of the estate. Echoes of my own footsteps cause my anxiety to spike. The shadows of the place move, sprawling across the grain of my stubble-coarse jawline. Willing my senses to sharpen beyond self awareness, my ears prick as I ignore the beat of my heart, the filling and emptying of my lungs.

Nothing.

Not a growl, nor the snap of a single branch beneath the claw of a Banshee. Still, my hands ball into fists, the obsidian pendant cooling against my skin, reminding me of the violent bloodlust that courses just beneath the surface.

The edge of the treeline is fast upon me, the hearty glow of a home warm against the onslaught of the season setting the sprawling lawns glistening in buttery oranges and yellows. The thin dusting of snow sparkles, trapping the light of the family home and making it crystalline beneath my boots as I plough onward, crushing it underfoot and not pausing to think on how long it has been since I sat before a roaring hearth of my own. My shaved head prickles with every stir of the breeze as I hurry, keen to get this over with.

I'm here on business, plain and simple. To deliver instructions to Adam Sinclair about a new offer Haedes has concocted in order to lure Demi back to him, and then return Mr. Sinclair's response to Mortaria.

It makes me exhausted, the emotional game they play with the poor woman, but it's not my business, and so I will adopt the role of messenger boy as usual. I suppose, if nothing else, it's a break from the constant wail of death, the explosive nature of carotid spray on sweat-slick skin.

My rubber soles meet with the gravel driveway, alabaster stones kicked up in my haste, crackling like tiny fireworks in the twilight. I hear him beyond the thick wood of the double doors, a break in the music that drifts through the cold, beckoning me, his bark echoing out against the familiar marble floors of the lobby. I continue to listen as the too-happy drone of a new yet familiar Christmas carol blares from the speakers right on cue, filling the chill silence of the expansive surrounding grounds.

Climbing the cocoa-coloured stone steps, I don't knock. Mainly because it's my duty to be here, and I require no show of hospitality. The wood grain is thick upon my palm as I enter, closing the door behind me fast and coming face to face with the base of a towering ladder.

I shimmy sideways, careful not to touch it despite my lack of grace. I'm far too used to battling, to using my weight and strength without thinking about it, to care much for my posture most of the time. The music continues to drown out my footsteps, the sound of Cerberus yapping almost totally diminished, too.

Angling my head, I gaze upward, turning on the spot to find the butler stringing golden tinsel from the central chandelier and pinning it to the curtain rails on either side of the door. It glints in the light, and yet I'm only reminded of gilded entrails.

"Hi." I wave, catching him off guard as my voice comes out deeper than I intend, the rumble of it echoing from the festively decorated walls. The ladder teeters as he startles, looking back over one shoulder at me and sighing loudly.

"Oh, it's you. You almost gave me a heart attack!" The butler's eyes bulge as he lets a piece of tinsel drop from his hand. It drapes itself artistically around the curtain rail as he descends the ladder, and I struggle not to roll my eyes.

The carol echoing out through the lobby reaches its crescendo, and then the music stops dead. Cerb's barking fills the silence immediately, frantic.

I tense, vein roped biceps pushing against the silk interior of my jacket as I inhale.

It's there, just barely, but it's there.

Smoke.

"Are you burning candles?" I demand of the butler, who turns to me, wiping his hands on the front of his pressed suit trousers.

"No. Why are you here?" he asks, getting right to the point as he places both hands, folded, in front of his well-polished belt buckle.

"To see him. Why else?" I ask rhetorically. He nods, thinning hair catches the light.

His eyes diminishing then, despite the warm glow from the enormous crystal chandelier projecting a rich hue across every surface and illuminating the floor with its flawless reflection.

Without another word he turns on the spot, posture perfect, soles but a whisper upon the marble floor. He leads me up the crimson sprawl of the velvet runner that falls the length of the stairs like a river of sanguine terror, feet a continual pitter pat despite the broadness of his shoulders and the clear bulk of his torso. I have often wondered about him, about his prior occupations, but again, it's not my business to ask, so I don't.

The corridor down which we travel is a blur of silken wallpaper and grandiose framed art that reeks of privileged pomposity. I let my eyes linger, if only slightly, on each one until we reach the Sinclair's master bedroom. Cerb is already there, scrapping at the wood, whining, making my heart increase in pace against my consent.

The butler reaches out and knocks, a waft of smoke filling my nostrils. I open my mouth to stop him, but he waits not even a moment before going to open the door.

"Shit!" he cusses, snatching his unsuspecting fingers back from the golden doorknob, a hiss of agony escaping him.

"Take him. Call 911." I spit, mind already whirring as adrenaline hits my system. Grabbing the enormous whimpering dog by the collar, I push him behind me defensively, blood pounding in my ears. The scent of smoke grows with every passing moment, but the butler stalls with predictable mortal impunity, hands visibly shaking.

"But..." I hear him stutter, so take a deep breath, allowing my mortal form to dissolve and the demon beneath to present, the seams of my leather jacket giving an audible rip as my muscles enlarge.

"Get out!" I growl, eyes glowing like hot embers stoked only by my desperation. I watch as the clementine hue lights his terrified face, before turning back to the door and listening to his hurried footfall disappear down the corridor as he drags the protesting Leonberger behind him.

I don't know what I expect to find inside, but I grit my teeth and grab the white-hot doorknob in my charred palm despite my mortal reservations, turning it and ignoring the pain. The starving blaze is immediately fuelled hotter and wilder as it sucks in air from the corridor behind me.

Now, and only now, the smoke detectors and fire alarms in the outer corridor go off, blaring loudly and causing me to jump as the devastating scene is revealed.

The flames are scarlet, rippling on both the ceiling and floor, an ocean of heat, of fire. I feel like I'm drowning in the smoke, the smoke that had been so contained that this monster had raged overhead without neither me nor the butler being any the wiser. I stand, shock rocking my stone-cold core.

The curtains, the bed, the armchairs that once surrounded the bay window are crackling, the wood of the antique armoire split open like a dry riverbed, nothing more than kindling for the hungry blaze. My face is lit, my eye sockets turned dark and hollow, my swirling tattoos dimmed in contrast.

Amongst it all, I find her.

She's cowering by the marble hearth. Perhaps the only part of the room that isn't ablaze, staring at two burning bodies.

Adam and Demi Sinclair.

Dead.

Her eyes are lit with fear, a fire so ferocious inside of them I have to wonder why she hasn't been reduced to bone and scorched flesh alongside her parents.

Standing, I blink once, then twice, deciding instantaneously that I must act, that I must risk myself to save the Sinclair girl.

For if I cannot save such innocence, what is it I'm doing tearing jaws asunder and snapping spinal cords down in hell? What am I fighting for?

My demonic-side snarls, wondering what sad sentimentalism has infected me. However, it should not fret. I have spent too long in The Ashen Waste, covered in ash, not snow, and surrounded by the death cries of demonic warfare, rather than the holy voices of a festive choir, to be anything other than damned.

The heat licks at my heels as I dart across the room, closing the distance between myself and the trembling redhead. The marble of the fireplace is warm to touch as I lean against it, hacking on the smoke drawn into my body against my consent.

She looks up at me among the blaze, eyes wide and full of tears, terror leaking down her face as her flushed cheeks struggle to suck in air. I can't say I blame her for her petrification at the sight of me. I can imagine my charred skin and glowing eyes are enough to give any child nightmares.

I bend down without hesitation, pulling her into my side as I slide a hand around her matchstick thin waist and hoist her up into my arms.

Looking left, then right, my eyes dart upward as a small glass chandelier falls to the burning carpet with a smash lost amid the undying crackle and roar. She flinches in my grasp at the sound, her body frail and shaking as she buries her face into my chest. Beneath, the stony crust of my demonic heart seems to crack, dissolved by the salt of her tears. Raw flesh thunders inside my ribcage as I find the door and walls now entirely consumed by the fire, the air becoming less tolerable with each passing second. The ceiling groans overhead, the tongues of the blaze sapping its strength.

I need to move.

"Hold on tight," I murmur into her hair, the scent of smoke and sweetness rising into my nostrils as her grip tightens on the leather collar of my jacket.

I lunge, seeing a break in the wall of flame and wasting no time on doubt or fear. I bound over the ashen corpse of Demi Sinclair, using the bed as a platform from which to propel myself. The frame creaks, then splinters beneath my demonic mass, but I am already leaping through the smoke and toward the door as it gives way right under my feet.

We reach the doorframe; her face still buried against my charred skin. The fire alarm wails. Sprinklers spray water in an icy torrent from the ceiling.

Yeah, because that's done a lot of good. I think to myself, shielding the child in my arms from the sudden faux rain, her body shuddering as a cough wracks through her fragile bones.

I carry her down the corridor, through the blaring alarms, smoke chasing us all the way to the landing where it plumes, climbing high like an elusive snake against the ceiling. It coils there, angry at being trapped, hungry for further destruction.

My thunderous tread echoes in my ears as I take the stairs two at a time, the runner bunching up beneath me and threatening to send me tumbling the length of the staircase. Christmas carols still drone out into the lobby, giving a grim and funereal holiness to the scene as choir boys croon *Silent Night* into the smoke.

Reaching the doors, I find the ladder lying abandoned on its side, tinsel scattered across the floor, an obstruction to my escape. With a last burst of power, I launch over the top of it, clutching the girl to me and skidding on my heels as I almost careen face first into the double doors.

My breathing is laboured as burst across the threshold and out of the house, the sound of Cerberus barking and whining at increasingly distant intervals the only sound.

I clutch the girl to me, the butler's eyes searching behind my silhouette for any other survivors.

I simply shake my head, and his eyes dart to the girl in my arms before they unceremoniously fill with tears.

"Oh, dear God..." he whispers before his mouth goes slack. In the distance, I can hear the approach of what I pray are fire engines.

The wail of the fire alarm, the scream of the sirens as they hurtle closer, Cerb's sudden howl, and the crooning soft power of the Christmas carols among it all paints an auditory picture I know I'll never forget as long as I live. Haunting and inescapably tragic.

As the moments tick on, I feel it begin. Small finger-tip-sized plunks of snow settling in my hair, on my skin. She shivers in my grasp, so light I've almost forgotten she's there, and I realise suddenly I'm standing stone-still upon the marble steps of the estate, unmoving.

I take a single step, almost mechanical as I glance at her bare feet slung over my elbow. They're riddled with goose-bumps, skin that had once been an angelic alabaster now charred with soot.

She peeks up at me from beneath her lashes as we stop atop the chill gravel. It's only now I realise I'm still a demon in a man's clothing, her skin lighting a warm shade of pumpkin beneath the glow of my molten irises.

I sigh, too aware that emergency services will be here soon, and try to relax, letting my heartbeat slow beneath her cheek and feeling my muscles diminish in size. I watch as the hands clutching the girl are once against masked by olive skin, and breathe deeply, wondering what exactly she must be think-ing.

Her face is shocked and confused as she watches me, so I pass her to the butler, removing my leather jacket from my shoulders and slinging it over her body to chase off the chill of the snowy evening.

I move to turn away, to leave without another word, but a small voice stops me.

"Don't go."

I spin back, slowly, finding her gaze curious and bright beneath the dark leather that's draped, enormous by comparison, over her trembling shoulders.

The butler looks down at her, surprise marring his face, but before he can respond I hear the approach of tyres squealing against the driveway. He looks at me, then back to the bundle of childish limbs and red hair in his arms.

"Can you just... hold her until I've dealt with them?" he requests, obviously nervous. I pucker my lips, and then wrinkle my nose, the cold beginning to seep into my biceps. I want to shake my head, to retreat, but she implores me with those eyes, and our gazes intermingle, warm among the cold blur of slow falling snowflakes.

I nod.

She reaches out for me, chubby hands and small delicate fingers protruding through the downfall of snow. I reach out too, taking her into my arms and making sure she remains tucked neatly inside my leather jacket.

I don't tell the butler what I'm going to do, don't speak another word as she gazes up at me with the kind of ignorant scrutiny that only a child can master. She's curious as she examines my face, now human and entirely unrecognisable from the demon I had been before.

I take several strides, climbing the stone stairs and sitting atop the highest step as the fire engine parks up and the sirens abruptly die. The crew clambers out as I position myself, legs sprawled down one side of the entryway, sheltered by the marble overhang casting me in shadow. Her body is a tangled mass of warmth and childish softness in my arms, her hair swept up by a chill and cruel breeze that won't seem to quit as night blankets the world around us.

"Are you... are you the devil?" she whispers to me.

I snort.

I wish I was the devil. She has a far nicer apartment, friends, and even a lover.

"Now, why would you ask that?" I enquire, keeping my voice low, like the rumble deep in the earth before a seismic shift occurs.

She doesn't look up at me as she replies.

"My friend Sandy Newman told me that the devil comes for girls with red hair..." she says absent-mindedly. Twirling a lock of blackened red strands around her index finger, her face is marred deeply with unwavering concentration.

"Your friend Sandy Newman is a twit," I reply, and she giggles. I fight a smile, but it lingers at the corners of my lips and refuses to let go.

"Oh, I know. I was just making sure." She is matter of fact as she finally looks up into my eyes, gaze blazing with all the seriousness accrued by women in their late forties. "So, if you're not the devil, are you Krampus?" she continues, wriggling in my arms so she's sitting on my lap rather than reclining. I scowl, her tiny elbows stabbing me in the ribs and causing me to wince.

"Krampus? What's Krampus?" I ask. Her eyes widen.

"You don't know who Krampus is?!" She puts her hand to her mouth, shocked as her almond-shaped eyes widen considerably.

"No. Should I?" I ask her, and she shrugs.

"Maybe. You're a grown-up, aren't you?" The question surprises me, as though she believes grown-ups are the equivalent of gods and that we aren't all just flailing around, unsure what the hell we're doing.

"Well, who told you about Krampus?" I enquire, eyes darting to the butler as he points furiously toward the upper floors. The firefighters have unloaded all their equipment now, and my conversation with the Sinclair girl halts while we wait for the thunderous onslaught of heroic footsteps to diminish as they enter the house.

"Well..." She puckers her mouth, a line of soot blemishing the fair skin of her chin.

"Was it Sandy Newman, by any chance?" I ask. She rolls her eyes, giving a tiny shiver as she tucks her hair behind one ear and bites down on the plump pink flesh of her bottom lip.

"Well, yes. But Krampus *is* real." She's defiant, thick lashes fluttering to increase the power of her certainty.

"Okay. Well then, tell me, what is Krampus?" I demand. She sighs a little.

"Krampus punishes bad kids. Instead of Santa bringing them presents, they get their asses beat." She looks guilty as the final part of this sentiment falls from her, but I can't help but laugh. Her scornful stare is enough to stop me fast though, her fists balling in the leather of my jacket.

"Why did you think I was Krampus?" I ask her, swallowing hard. She suddenly looks sad, her eyes dropping to her leather draped knees.

"I'm a bad kid. My daddy... he wanted me to say goodbye, but I didn't want to. He always leaves, and it's nearly Christmas. He said we could decorate the tree tomorrow. He *promised*. Now—" Her eyes fill with tears as her body goes rigid with shock.

"Hey, hey. Don't cry. It's not your fault. I'm — I'm sorry," I stutter, suddenly shattered by the tear-stained gaze of this unexpectedly charismatic six-year-old.

"I got mad. I was—" she begins, but before she can finish the sentence, her bottom lip starts to tremble. Moments later, she breaks down entirely and begins to sob in my arms.

I hold her for a while, feeling her pain as the shock rolls over her small childish body and then surges in fresh waves of grief.

I've never lost a parent, but I lost my home over and over again. Then again, I haven't seen my mother in years. She's probably long gone. The thought of this loss shocks me, though I know it shouldn't. If she is still alive, she'd be extremely old. She probably wouldn't even recognise me.

When I was a child, she was paranoid, scared of the system, the government. She said they were out to get us, to get me. Some people said she was crazy, but what do they know? Perhaps she knew something I didn't. Perhaps she knew about my demon-half all along.

I spent my entire childhood saying goodbye to one school after another, always being the new kid, the kid with the weird mom who worked cash in hand odd-jobs and refused to use her social security number. We barely scraped by, barely lived, really, but I loved her. She was the only home I've ever known.

I miss her every day. Miss the brown-bagged peanut butter and jelly sandwiches that made my hands sticky because she always used too much jelly. Miss the repetitive, banal safety of poverty and how even though, deep down, I knew we had nothing; I was all she needed. I always knew everything would be alright as long as we had each other.

It makes me want to know if she's still alive.

I ponder on this in silence as the girl's body trembles against the steel certainty of my own, the chill whipping around us despite my attempt at shelter.

As I hold her close to me, pulling the jacket up tight around her throat to keep away the cold, an ambulance appears at the end of the drive, sirens blaring. She startles, peeking out from where she's left a small tear-stained puddle on the black cotton of my t-shirt. I realise, as the noise grates on my nerves, that I've relaxed my killing instincts for the first time in years. I hadn't even heard it approaching, too lost in nostalgic reverie.

"Persephone, sweetie. Come here." The butler calls for the girl in my arms, and I realise I hadn't even bothered to ask her name.

The choice of name isn't lost on me either. Perhaps it was a cruel joke by Adam, meant to spite Haedes.

I mean, we all know the myth, the stories the Muses had spun about a goddess named Persephone being the sole weakness of The God of the Underworld, but there's no actual truth to it.

It was a cruel prank to highlight the fact no God or Goddess would ever look twice at Haedes. Not without pissing off Zeus and earning themselves one hell of a reputation— or so I'd gleaned from the few dinners I attended as security and what Luce told me. Haedes was, and still is, the unlovable black sheep of Rhea's blessed sons. They told the story of his kidnapping a woman to serve his need, his desperation for company, to hurt him the only way they knew how.

As I'm musing on this, the girl, Persephone, is watching me even still. She's expectant, and it's not until she's blinked a few times I realise she's barefoot and is soundlessly asking me to carry her.

I obey, helpless to say no, rising from the stone of the steps with a silent and stoic air and carrying her to the ambulance. Here, a paramedic is waiting by gleaming white backdoors that hang open, exposing a host of medical equipment and a gurney bathed in stark light.

"We just want to check her out," the male paramedic assures me, his eyes softening as I get closer to him. He's shorter than me by several inches, and my shadow casts darkness upon his face, turning the blacks of his eyes dark with fear.

It's then I realise I'm clutching her, physically cradling her to me like she's the most precious thing in the world. The butler cocks his head, eyes narrowing as the child continues to stare up at me, mouth unmoving.

"Sir, you need to let go—" The paramedic stutters, his bottle-green jumpsuit not at all flattering beneath his puffy parka.

Reluctantly, I nod, handing the leather-swathed girl to him with as much care and grace as I can muster.

Once he takes her meagre weight from my arms, the chill of the night immediately embraces me, causing me to give an abrupt shudder.

The paramedic sweeps Persephone behind the vehicle, the lights on its roof still flashing scarlet and azure across my face and the surrounding lawns at unceasing intervals.

"Thank you. For what you did." The butler's voice startles me, his hand coming up to rest on the back of my broad shoulder, a warm patch amongst the chill.

"It was nothing." I shrug, but I hear him clear his throat.

"Jules. Please, call me Jules. I've had you wrong, Xion. I know why he sends you here, Haedes. It's because you're a monster—but I also failed to see that you're a man." Turning to him, surprise transforms my face, eyebrows rising fast on my forehead.

I stare into his face, pulse quickening as I take a quick note of my surroundings and my muscles disturb the frozen tears that soak my shirt. Panic clutches me. That he might see the weak man I try so hard to ignore, to forget I'd once been.

The unknowing killer within who seduced an innocent and then gutted her at the moment she finally gave herself over fully in body and soul.

The mortal in me is the bait, demon the snare. I know I'm not ugly. I could lure in any number of women. This only makes my existence even more despicable, even more unforgivable.

I was built to hunt the innocent.

Sighing, I realise my mistake. After so long of being the snare, I've returned to my angelic appearance, my smile and heroism only bait for a waiting trap.

I've let my guard down because of the girl.

"Forget about it. Really. Moment of weakness," I brush off his sentiment like the snow dissolving fast upon my scalp. His expression turns cold, mouth pressing into a dissatisfied and thin line as his lips drain of blood.

"And here I was thinking it was a moment of strength. I know Persephone won't forget what you did—" he replies, expression sad.

I shake my head without realising what it is I'm doing.

I hope she doesn't remember.

Of this day, it's not only her trauma I wish she'd forget, but my demonic face as well. People like me have no place in the memory of a child, so I can only hope that shock and age rob her of the terror this night has brought, that the nothingness left in its place will serve as a balm to soothe her festering grief.

"I have to go," I mutter, heart suddenly frantic beneath my ribs.

The mortal world is no place for me, not any longer.

Without waiting for any kind of dismissal or acknowledgement from Jules, I wander back across the lawns, looking back only once to find smoke rising high into the air. It's acrid, singing my nostrils even still and carrying with it the undeniable scent of death, of burning human meat.

I turn from the destruction, from the flashing lights and blaring sirens of this snow-scattered night, picking my way back towards The Hollow as panic rises thick and noxious in my gut.

Balling my fists, I know it is time that I return to The Ashen Waste, to the killing fields. It's time I remember and accept who I truly am.

A Monster.

Coming here was a mistake. Even if I did save the life of that child... Persephone.

I thought I was done with my mortality, thought I lost it beneath the thick layers of charred flesh and molten tattoos that have made up my physical appearance for most of the last decade.

Turns out, it isn't as easy to rid myself of the mortality within after all. I'm doomed to suffer, unlovable, with the guilt of a heavy burden on my back, crippling me more with every step.

Except —

The child looked at me with kindness. Her gaze melting my frosty reserve, her curiosity cracking the stone walls encasing my heart.

I have *felt* for the first time in forever. Experienced what it means to be human and alive.

It wasn't a Christmas miracle that caused this shift, either.

All it took was the harrowing call of a festive choir among the silence of the dead, a tiny orphan's unwavering gaze, and a touch of smoke and snow.

ALSO BY

#8 Violet Dawn

#9 Lavender Storm

CONCLUDING NOVEL

#10 QUEENS OF FANTASY (Anticipated 2024)

QUEENS OF FANTASY SHORTS AND NOVELLAS

TIDAL KISS SHORTS AND NOVELLAS

#0.5 Beyond The Shallows

#3.5 Waiting For Gideon

#3.75 Vexed

ASHEN TOUCH SHORTS AND NOVELLAS

#4.25 Death Blooms - (Releasing February 2024)

#4.5 A Touch Of Smoke And Snow

AETHERIAL EMBRACE SHORTS AND NOVELLAS

#9.25 Ambrosia Nights

OTHER GENRES FROM KRISTY NICOLLE

DYSTOPIAN ROMANCE:

Something Blue- A Dystopian Romance Standalone

POETRY:

I Am Arcana- A Tarot Inspired Poetry Collection

Starsong- A Zodiac Inspired Poetry Collection

To keep up to date with the latest release dates, spin offs, and exclusive content, head on over to kristynicolle.com

ABOUT THE AUTHOR

30-Year-Old British Author of Award-Winning Indie Fantasy
Romance, Kristy Nicolle is escaping the pain of Ehlers Danlos
Syndrome by crafting intricate and immersive worlds for her
readers. She lives in Norwich, Norfolk, with her long-time
life partner Mark, and can often be found writing in her local
coffee shop - *Botany and Beans,* with a peppermint mocha,

surrounded by beloved witchy paraphernalia and plants she knows only too well she'd kill at home.

SCAN THE QR CODE WITH YOUR PHONE CAMERA FOR SO-CIAL MEDIA LINKS